THE

GHOST
HUNTER'S

HANDBOOK

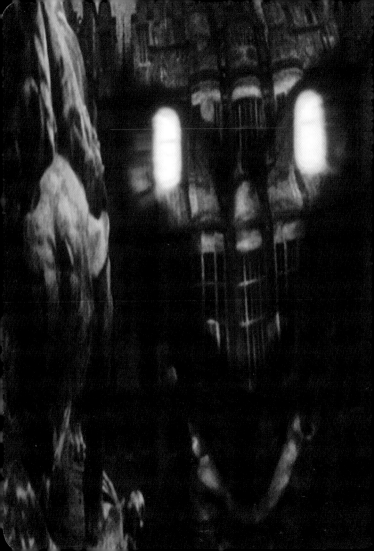

THE

GHOST HUNTER'S

HANDBOOK

by Lori Summers

PSS!
PRICE STERN SLOAN

Copyright © 2002 by Quirk Productions

Illustrations copyright © 2002 by Headcase Design

www.quirkproductions.com

Designed by Paul Kepple and Timothy Crawford @ Headcase Design
Layout by Hotfoot Studio

Published by Price Stern Sloan, a division of Penguin Putnam Books for Young Readers, 345 Hudson Street, New York, NY 10014

PSS! is a registered trademark of Penguin Putnam Inc.

Printed in Singapore.

Library of Congress Control Number: 2002104249

ISBN: 0-8431-4916-7

A B C D E F G H I J

PHOTOGRAPHY CREDITS

pg. ii: Photofest

pg. x: Photofest

pg. 8: Photofest

pg. 10: PhotoDisc

pg. 13: PhotoDisc

pg. 22: Photofest

pg. 41 (top): RAF

pg. 42: Photofest

pg. 58: Photofest

pg. 72: Photofest

pg. 74: Photofest

pg. 77: Photofest

pg. 78: Photofest

CONTENTS

INTRODUCTION

Have you ever seen a ghost? Have you ever had the feel-ing that you weren't alone, even when no one was with you? Have you ever heard unexplained noises, or had the feeling you were being watched while walking past a graveyard? Have you ever seen something that appeared out of thin air and vanished just as suddenly? Then maybe you have seen—or at least been near—a ghost!

An experience like this doesn't have to be scary. It can be fun. If you've seen or heard a ghost, were you excited? Thrilled? Maybe a little freaked out? Does the idea of see-ing ghosts up close and personal make you curious? What are they, and where did they come from? If you'd like to find some answers to these questions, you may have the makings of a ghost hunter. Can you study ghosts the way you'd study math, art, or reading? Yes, you can . . . but not in a classroom—and the good thing is, there aren't any spelling lists in the homework. This book is the best place to begin.

People have told ghost stories for probably as long as they've been telling stories. Almost every town in the world has its own version of a haunted house—and you only need to go as far as the Internet to read thousands of stories told by people who believe they have had an encounter with a ghost.

But are they really encountering ghosts? Or are they just easily scared? That's where this handbook comes in handy. It contains all the information you'll need to figure out whether you're dealing with a ghostly infestation or just a drafty, creaky old house. That's what professional ghost hunters, or "parapsychologists," do. You might have been thinking that a ghost hunter tries to capture ghosts, or eliminate them, or drive them away. But what ghost hunters are hunting aren't ghosts, precisely, but real, concrete evidence that ghosts exist.

There are many, many personal stories of ghosts, but there's no real scientific evidence—yet—that they're real. This handbook will show you how to observe and gather that evidence. In one sense, a ghost hunter is a little bit like a bird-watcher. His job is to observe a ghost, record it, and maybe even communicate with it! If that sounds like fun, read on and find out how it's done.

AS WITH MORTALS, THE APPEARANCE OF GHOSTS CAN VARY WIDELY;
FOR EXAMPLE, SOME ARE BETTER DRESSERS THAN OTHERS.

WHAT IS A GHOST?

Lots of people claim to have seen a ghost. But what, exactly, are they talking about? A floating, misty vapor? A disembodied voice? A weird knocking sound in the walls? It would be useful to have a better definition.

Most people who use the word "ghost" mean the soul, spirit, or essence of a dead person that remains in the world of the living in one form or another. But within that general definition, there are a few special kinds of spooks, such as *poltergeists* and *apparitions*. Even animals may come back as ghosts!

The idea that a person's soul survives death is not new. In fact, it's a belief that many people share. Although there is no scientific proof, that doesn't mean you can't believe it. Whether you believe in the afterlife or not is a personal decision. Many ghost hunters work toward the day when they can explain the existence of ghosts using the laws of science. History is full of examples of phenomena that were thought to be magical or otherworldly and then turned out to have a scientific explanation. Ghosts may turn out the same way. In any case, what you're after is proof that they exist. We can leave it to the scientists to explain *why* they exist.

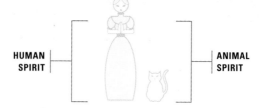

HUMAN
SPIRIT

ANIMAL
SPIRIT

GENERAL GHOST CHARACTERISTICS

Although the various types of ghosts can be very different, there are some general characteristics that ghost hunters have noted throughout the years:

Translucency: If the ghost is one that can be seen (some can only be heard or felt), usually it is translucent, which means that you can see partially through it. Ghost observers may at first think they are seeing a regular person, until they realize they can see things behind their visitor!

Insubstantiality: This means that the ghost has no physical substance. You can't touch and feel it like you would another person—and if you tried, your hand would pass right through! You may be able to see or hear the ghost, but it doesn't take a solid form. It's almost like fog—you can see it, but you can't hold onto it.

Dropping Temperature: Many ghost observers have noticed that when a ghost is present, the temperature in the vicinity drops, often dramatically. It can get cold enough that people nearby can see their breath! Some experts think that this happens because the ghost uses the heat in the air to make itself seen or heard (because heat is a kind of energy) and as a result, the air grows colder. Whatever the reason, it pays to be aware of sudden chills.

Repetition: Many ghosts seem compelled to repeat the same actions over and over again. They can be seen walking the same hallway in the house where they died, or can be heard repeating the same words to different observers. Some will revisit the same location time and again, but other types of ghosts appear in a particular location just once.

WHAT IS A HAUNTING?

We've all heard stories of haunted houses. Most towns seem to have their own legends of an old creepy mansion where a resident ghost makes a nuisance of itself, and scares away anyone who tries to live there. But what does it really mean when a place is haunted?

A ghost can appear anywhere, but when an entity shows up repeatedly at one specific location, that place is said to be "haunted." Any place can be haunted: There are cases of haunted fields, haunted streets, and even haunted vehicles. Any place that has a ghost that visits regularly can be described as haunted, be it a doghouse or a phone booth! Even a person can be haunted (see "Poltergeists" in Chapter 2).

GHOST FACT OR FICTION: QUIZ

There are lots of myths about ghosts. Take this quiz to test your ghost knowledge quotient.

(T)	(F)	1.	Ghosts carry long chains that they rattle.
(T)	(F)	2.	Ghosts drape themselves in white sheets.
(T)	(F)	3.	Ghosts moan and wail.
(T)	(F)	4.	Ghosts float.
(T)	(F)	5.	Ghosts hang out in cemeteries.
(T)	(F)	6.	Ghosts say "boo!"
(T)	(F)	7.	Only people can come back as ghosts.

(1) **False:** This popular image may have originated in Charles Dickens's famous tale *A Christmas Carol*, in which the ghost of Jacob Marley visits his old colleague Ebenezer Scrooge to warn him his soul is in danger. Marley's ghost is draped in long chains, the chains of selfishness he forged in life. So far as ghost experts know, Marley's ghost was the only chain rattler in existence!

(2) **False:** The only ghost likely to be wearing a sheet is a faux ghost—someone dressed up for Halloween, that is! Most ghosts appear wearing the same kinds of clothes that they wore in life, if not the exact outfit they were dressed in when they died or were buried.

3. **False:** Some ghosts make no noise at all, while others can talk or even sing—but moaning and wailing? Not likely. The noises most often heard in haunted houses are footsteps, knocking or rapping on the walls, and regular human voices. If a ghost is seen directly, most of the time it is silent. Many ghosts have been seen with their lips moving as if they're speaking, but no sound comes out.

4. **True . . . and false:** Ghosts can indeed float—but they can also walk, run, jump, and even ride a horse—pretty much all the movements they could do in life. They may walk with an other-worldly smoothness that seems like floating, but ghosts are usually free to move however they like.

5. **True . . . and false:** While ghosts can sometimes be found at or near cemeteries, the most commonly haunted places are homes. The spirit of a dead person will usually hang around where it feels an emotional connection. Unless it has some special reason for wanting to haunt its grave (like the Headless Horseman of Sleepy Hollow, who was trying to unite his head and body—see pages 14–15) or its grave has been disturbed (in which case the ghost may be angry and want the grave restored to its formerly quiet state), the ghost is likelier to pick a more pleasant spot to haunt.

6. **False:** People say "boo." Ghosts say whatever they want to!

7. **False:** Ghosts are usually the specters of people, but there have been instances of hauntings by the spirits of animals, too. Some people have reported encountering ghosts that didn't seem to ever have been living beings, just shapeless masses of energy or mist—but those could just have been aliens (see *The UFO Hunter's Handbook*).

There are many famous haunted places throughout the world. Some of the most haunted spots would never have made it on a map if it hadn't been for their resident spook. Here are a few of the more infamous hauntings. Keep in mind that these are famous hauntings, not necessarily ones that are generally believed by ghost hunters.

HOUSE OF HORROR: AMITYVILLE

In late 1975, George and Kathleen Lutz and their three young children moved into their dream home on Ocean Avenue in Amityville, New York. Less than a month later they fled the house in terror, leaving behind everything they owned.

Each family member reported having been frightened by strange noises and weird voices. Even scarier, they were noticing dramatic personality changes in each other. Their story is told in the book *The Amityville*

Horror, by Jay Anson, which was made into a popular (and scary) film. It turned out that a murder had taken place in the house not long before the Lutzes bought it. That fact alone isn't always enough to cause a haunting, but the house was also built on land that was once a Native American burial ground. With so many restless and disgruntled spirits nearby, that house was just begging to be haunted!

GHOST SHIP: THE LADY LUVIBUND

On the evening of February 13, 1748, just-married Captain Simon Reed and his bride sailed away from the coast of Kent (in southeastern England) on the *Lady Luvibund*. The newlyweds went belowdecks to celebrate with friends and crew. Abovedecks, shortly thereafter, first mate John Rivers, maddened with jealousy, bashed the helmsman over the head, took control of the ship, and deliberately drove her onto the Goodwin Sands, a treacherous area of sandbars. By morning there was no trace of the *Lady Luvibund*.

Fifty years later to the day, on the same stretch of coastline, Captain James Westlake saw an old-fashioned schooner bearing down on his ship; as it passed by—dangerously close—he heard the sounds of merrymaking. Later that day, a fishing boat saw the same schooner break up on the Sands—but when they went to help, there was no trace of the ship or her crew. Since then, every fifty years on February 13, the *Lady Luvibund* is said to relive her tragic voyage.

GOVERNMENT GHOST: THE WHITE HOUSE

One of the most famous haunted buildings in the United States is the White House. Yes, despite all the Secret Service's efforts to keep out uninvited guests, ghosts routinely visit its rooms. It probably started with Abraham Lincoln, who was interested in the supernatural—his wife, Mary Todd Lincoln, is said to have arranged for séances to be held in the White House. About ten days before Lincoln died, he had a dream in which he saw himself in a coffin—he told people that he had dreamed that he had been assassinated.

On April 14, 1865, he was shot by John Wilkes Booth. For years afterward, people reported hearing ghostly footsteps around the White House. Grace Coolidge, wife of Calvin Coolidge, the thirtieth president, claimed to have seen the ghostly figure of Lincoln staring out of the Oval Office. When Queen Wilhelmina of the Netherlands stayed at the White House, she reported that upon hearing a knock on her bedroom door, she opened it and encountered the apparition of Lincoln.

The room is known as the Lincoln Bedroom. Many others have reported seeing the ghost in or near the room. Perhaps he still thinks of it as his own room—you'd get upset, too, if strangers kept sleeping in your bedroom.

MULTIPLE HAUNTINGS: PENGERSICK CASTLE

Pengersick Castle, in Cornwall, England, is almost a textbook case of a haunted house: it's very old, it has a violent history, and lots of people have passed through it. The original owner of the castle, Henry Pengersick, was said to have been an angry man with a particular dislike for members of the clergy. In fact, he attacked not one, but two of them—beating up a local vicar and killing a monk from a nearby abbey. In the years after Henry's death, the castle passed through many hands and strange tales abounded. The groundskeeper at the castle said that he felt something brush by him in the garden, then was overcome by the smell of incense. A neighbor soon reported seeing a ghostly figure of a monk in a long, hooded robe walk right through his garden wall!

On another occasion, a visitor to the castle was sitting quietly by the fire when a black dog with red eyes suddenly appeared next to him. The crimson-eyed animal has appeared so frequently that locals have given it a name: "devil's hound."

GHOSTS UNDERGROUND: A SUBWAY HAUNTING

This incident occurred in Toronto, Ontario, Canada, where a subway tunnel runs through Hogg's Hollow, an area that was once a riverbed. Five hundred years ago, before the valley was settled by Europeans, it was the site of a fierce battle between the Iroquois and the Huron. After the battle, a heavy downpour turned the riverbanks into mud, and many of the fallen warriors were washed away before their bodies could receive a proper burial.

One autumn night in the early 1990s, three subway maintenance workers were sent to make a repair in a tunnel after the last train had departed. As they approached the worksite, they heard voices. Drawing closer, they realized the voices were chanting—but the words they heard were not English or French. One of the repairmen, a native Canadian, stopped suddenly and exclaimed that he understood some of the words—they were in an old language he had heard his grandfather speak, and they were a prayer for the dead.

The workers immediately called the station to see if anyone else had been given permission to enter the tunnel—but they were told that no other crews were there. When the workers reached the repair site, the chanting stopped. They fixed the problem and quickly walked away. As they did, they heard the unmistakable sound of beating drums.

WHERE THE GHOSTS ARE

So how does a place become haunted? Most of the usual reasons go back to the theory that ghosts are the returned souls of people who should have passed on to the next world but are still hanging around this one. This is why the ghosts tend to stick to places they know well, or to which they have a strong emotional connection. Many times, ghosts haunt the places where they died, especially if they died a violent or traumatic death. Other times, a ghost may return to a place where it was happiest, or a place where the people it cared about in life still live.

In *The Legend of Sleepy Hollow*, for example, as told by Washington Irving, a ghost known as the Headless Horseman rides his phantom horse along the road from an old Revolutionary war battleground to the local cemetery—all the while carrying his head under his arm! Legend told that the horseman had lost his head in battle, and was on a ghostly mission to reunite it with his body.

In another case, a battleship was haunted by several different ghosts. The ghost hunter who investigated found out that all the men who were haunting the ship had served aboard her in life, although none of them had died aboard the ship.

One very common site for hauntings is land that was once a burial ground. Because old cemeteries are often in prime real estate locations, developers sometimes choose these sites for new houses, shopping malls, or even amusement parks—but it's not a good idea! In such cases, the specters' attachment isn't to the new building, but to the ground where their bones lie. The headstones and the visible part of the cemetery may be gone, but the bones of the dead are still beneath the ground, and the spirits

GHOSTS AROUND THE WORLD

1. **ALBANIA**
   lugat
2. **CHINA**
   gui
3. **CZECH REPUBLIC**
   strasidlo
4. **DENMARK**
   spogelse
5. **HOLLAND**
   zweem
6. **ICELAND**
   draugur
7. **IRELAND**
   taibhse
8. **ITALY**
   fantasma, spettro
9. **JAPAN**
   yuurei
10. **KENYA**
    kizuka
11. **PHILIPPINES**
    multo
12. **SAUDI ARABIA**
    jinn
13. **SOUTH AFRICA**
    isipoki
14. **SPAIN**
    fantasma, espectro
15. **TURKEY**
    hortlak

EUROPE

AFRICA

SOUTH AMERICA

North Atlantic Ocean

South Atlantic Ocean

60°   0°

0°

might not be too thrilled about having something built above their resting place.

So what sorts of buildings are especially prone to becoming haunted? Here are some characteristics to watch for:

• **Old buildings.** The longer the building has been standing, the more likely it is to be haunted. If it has been around for centuries, it just may be that something

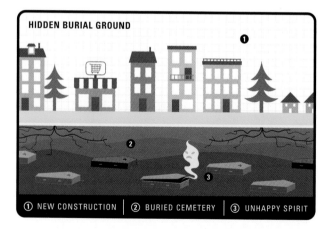

HIDDEN BURIAL GROUND

① NEW CONSTRUCTION | ② BURIED CEMETERY | ③ UNHAPPY SPIRIT

violent or traumatic happened there that could inspire a haunting.

• **Lots of inhabitants or visitors.** Buildings where people come and go a lot are more prone to hauntings, because the chances are greater that something traumatic happened to one of those people—or because of one of them! For this reason, you'll find a lot of restaurants, hotels, inns, boardinghouses, and clubs on any list of haunted houses.

• **Unusual or historic location.** If the building rests on land where dramatic events have occurred, there's a good chance it could be haunted. For example, an old battlefield is an excellent place to watch for ghosts, but not such a good choice for a new mini-golf course. You might find yourself trying to putt through the ghost of a fallen soldier!

FIELD GUIDE TO GHOSTS

Ghosts, specters, ghouls, apparitions, poltergeists . . . a ghost hunter could get confused by all the different labels. Many ghost hunters find it useful to classify ghosts based on their apparent purpose in returning from the dead. There are four main types of spirits: mischief-makers, avengers, message-bringers, and haunters.

MISCHIEF-MAKERS

These entities seem to be hanging about just to cause trouble. Most mischief-makers are poltergeists, although other ghosts can misbehave, too. What is a poltergeist? The word is German for "noisy ghost," and that's just what it is. A poltergeist is almost always invisible: rarely will the witness see a floating image or a misty vapor. Instead, all that can be seen is what the poltergeist does—which is usually to throw things and make a lot of noise. A mild-mannered poltergeist might only make minor mischief— like moving someone's keys from where they were last placed, or knocking on the walls or windows in the middle of the night. An aggressive poltergeist, on the other hand, can turn the contents of a whole house upside down, blast the stereo through the night, or even steal a car—much to the surprise of the home's living occupants.

Poltergeists typically do not attempt to communicate with the living, nor do they seem emotionally connected to their place of haunting. They may cause chaos and even damage, but they do not intentionally harm those around them. Having a poltergeist around is a bit like having an annoying neighbor who shows up once in awhile, breaks things, and won't leave until he's good and ready.

Poltergeist activity is sometimes centered on a person—usually a teenager or someone experiencing intense emotions. Ghost experts believe the increased level of emotional energy may fuel the poltergeist, allowing it to play pranks. Some researchers argue, however, that the person may unknowingly be causing the disturbances him- or herself. Their theory is that the poltergeist activity—objects moving about by themselves—is caused by the affected person's own strong emotions. The ability to move

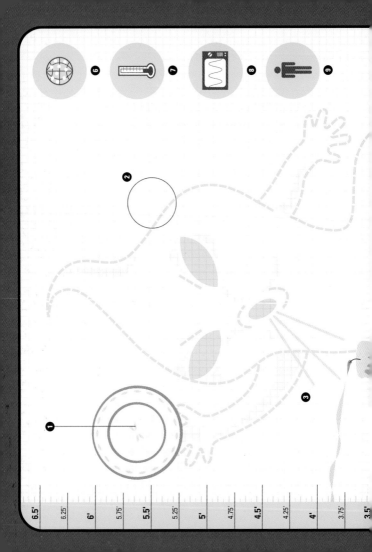

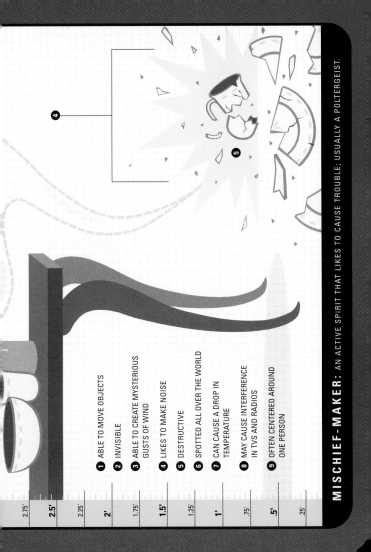

1 ABLE TO MOVE OBJECTS

2 INVISIBLE

3 ABLE TO CREATE MYSTERIOUS GUSTS OF WIND

4 LIKES TO MAKE NOISE

5 DESTRUCTIVE

6 SPOTTED ALL OVER THE WORLD

7 CAN CAUSE A DROP IN TEMPERATURE

8 MAY CAUSE INTERFERENCE IN TVS AND RADIOS

9 OFTEN CENTERED AROUND ONE PERSON

MISCHIEF-MAKER: AN ACTIVE SPIRIT THAT LIKES TO CAUSE TROUBLE; USUALLY A POLTERGEIST.

2.75'
2.5'
2.25'
2'
1.75'
1.5'
1.25'
1'
.75'
.5'
.25'

things with one's mind is called "psychokinesis" (sy-ko-kihn-EE-sis). People with this ability can learn to control it.

A famous literary poltergeist is Peeves, a character in the Harry Potter series, who whooshes through the hallways of the Hogwarts School of Witchcraft and Wizardry, throwing things at the students and taunting them whenever they pass his way. Another well-known poltergeist is Beetlejuice, the title character from the movie of the same name, who gets his thrills from playing tricks not only on living people, but also on his fellow spooks.

AVENGERS

Many ghosts appear to have returned from the afterlife in order to right a wrong done to them, or even to someone else, in life. Sometimes a ghost may wish to bring a crime to light, so that those in the world of the living may right the wrongdoing. Quite often a ghost's goal is to avenge his or her own death, either by revealing the culprit so that earthly justice may be done or by personally retaliating against the murderer.

Avenging ghosts can make themselves known by various means. Some are merely apparitions, which are ghosts that can appear to living beings, but cannot speak. Apparitions may try to communicate by other means, such as repeatedly appearing in the very place where they died. An apparition might continue to make itself visible to various people in the world of the living until one of them realizes that there might have been some foul play regarding the apparition's death!

Other avengers can talk, and therefore inspire a living person to help them exact revenge. A good example is the ghost of Hamlet's father, who makes a dramatic

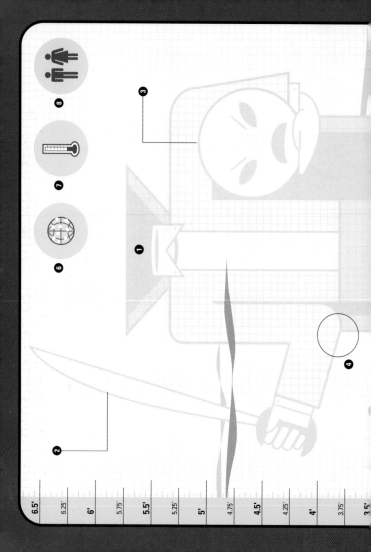

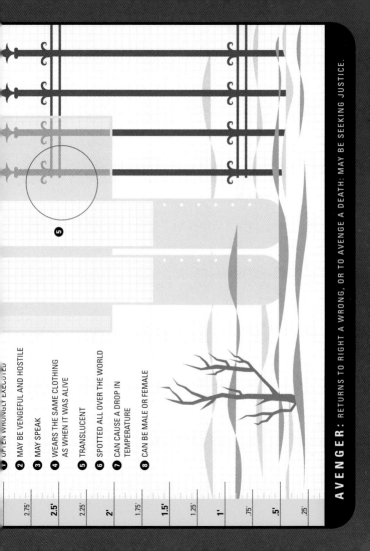

1. OFTEN WRONGLY EXECUTED
2. MAY BE VENGEFUL AND HOSTILE
3. MAY SPEAK
4. WEARS THE SAME CLOTHING AS WHEN IT WAS ALIVE
5. TRANSLUCENT
6. SPOTTED ALL OVER THE WORLD
7. CAN CAUSE A DROP IN TEMPERATURE
8. CAN BE MALE OR FEMALE

5

2.75'
2.5'
2.25'
2'
1.75'
1.5'
1.25'
1'
.75'
.5'
.25'

AVENGER: RETURNS TO RIGHT A WRONG, OR TO AVENGE A DEATH; MAY BE SEEKING JUSTICE.

appearance at the beginning of William Shakespeare's play *Hamlet*. Hamlet, who is the prince of Denmark, has been alerted by some very frightened guards to the repeated nighttime visitations of a shade who looks like his father. This ghost will speak only to his son, Hamlet, and commands him to take revenge for this "murther most foul." Insistent, the ghost wails from offstage until Hamlet agrees to the task!

A ghost's method of exacting revenge is to make life unpleasant for someone who they feel deserves it. A good example of this kind of ghost is Sam Wheat, the ghostly character played by Patrick Swayze in the film *Ghost*. After he is murdered—by his own best friend!—Sam's spirit stays behind to avenge his murder and to protect his fiancée from harm. With the help of a "medium"—that is, a person who can communicate with the world of the dead—and from some fellow ghosts, who show him a few tricks for manipulating the material world, Sam brings his killer to justice. When all is made right in this world, Sam is able to pass on to the next world.

MESSAGE-BRINGERS

Many ghosts hang around to deliver a message. One type of ghost appears either at the moment of death, or soon after. Ghost expert Michael White calls these ghosts "crisis apparitions." A crisis apparition may appear as a vision to a witness at the same time that the real person is miles away. Many people have reported seeing visions of a friend or loved one at the exact moment of that person's death, even though the witness and the dying person are separated by long distances. Sometimes a person who recently passed away will appear in ghostly form to bring a loved one a message of reassurance and comfort.

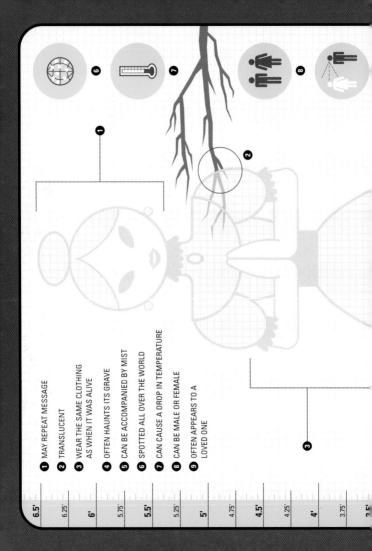

1. MAY REPEAT MESSAGE
2. TRANSLUCENT
3. WEAR THE SAME CLOTHING AS WHEN IT WAS ALIVE
4. OFTEN HAUNTS ITS GRAVE
5. CAN BE ACCOMPANIED BY MIST
6. SPOTTED ALL OVER THE WORLD
7. CAN CAUSE A DROP IN TEMPERATURE
8. CAN BE MALE OR FEMALE
9. OFTEN APPEARS TO A LOVED ONE

6.5'
6.25'
6'
5.75'
5.5'
5.25'
5'
4.75'
4.5'
4.25'
4'
3.75'
3.5'

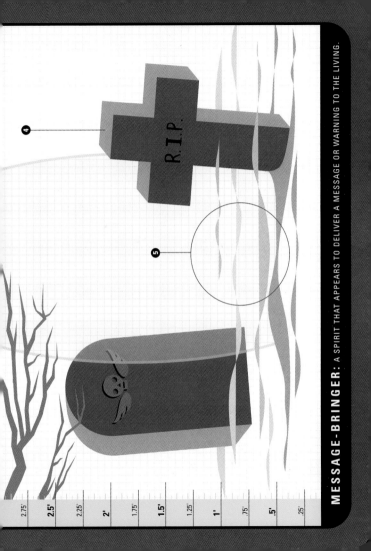

R.I.P.

MESSAGE-BRINGER: A SPIRIT THAT APPEARS TO DELIVER A MESSAGE OR WARNING TO THE LIVING.

Other ghosts may be trying to bring an important secret into the open, or to warn the living of impending danger. They may say the same thing repeatedly until they find someone (in the world of the living) who will listen. The ghost of Jacob Marley (the original chain-rattling ghost mentioned in Chapter 1) was a message-bringer. In Charles Dickens's *A Christmas Carol*, wealthy Ebenezer Scrooge is a miserly and miserable old man. Luckily for him, the ghost of his old colleague Jacob Marley, who must suffer in the afterlife for his selfish behavior when he was alive, cares enough to try to help Scrooge reform before it's too late.

HAUNTERS

Finally, we come to haunters, which are the least compli-cated of the ghost types. Haunters hang around specific places to which they feel so attached that they just can't say goodbye even though they're dead! They may simply feel a fond attachment to the place or something important may have happened to them there.

Haunters may or may not interact with the living. Some of them just want to stay where they were happiest—the ghostly sailors on the battleship in Chapter 1 are a good example. There have been several reports of musical ghosts who loved their instruments so much that they came back from the dead to play them again! Others want to protect a place or the people in it. In the TV show *The Ghost and Mrs. Muir*, the ghostly naval captain Daniel Greeg loves his little cottage so deeply that he cannot leave it, and continues to look after the place even after Mrs. Muir and her two children move in one hundred years later.

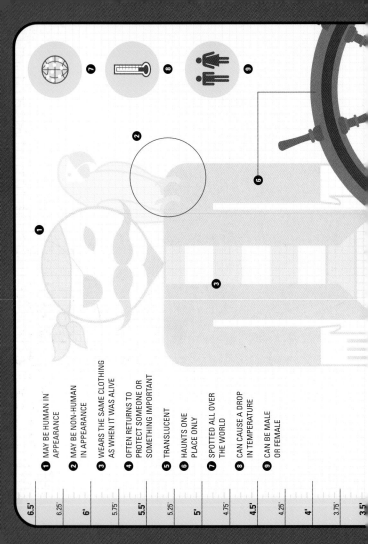

1 MAY BE HUMAN IN APPEARANCE

2 MAY BE NON-HUMAN IN APPEARANCE

3 WEARS THE SAME CLOTHING AS WHEN IT WAS ALIVE

4 OFTEN RETURNS TO PROTECT SOMEONE OR SOMETHING IMPORTANT

5 TRANSLUCENT

6 HAUNTS ONE PLACE ONLY

7 SPOTTED ALL OVER THE WORLD

8 CAN CAUSE A DROP IN TEMPERATURE

9 CAN BE MALE OR FEMALE

6.5'
6.25'
6'
5.75'
5.5'
5.25'
5'
4.75'
4.5'
4.25'
4'
3.75'
3.5'

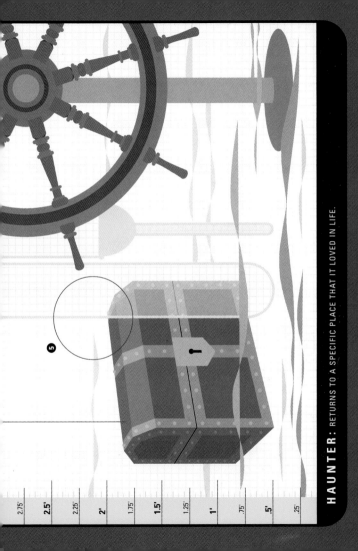

2.75'
2.5'
2.25'
2'
1.75'
1.5'
1.25'
1'
.75'
.5'
.25'

⑤

HAUNTER: RETURNS TO A SPECIFIC PLACE THAT IT LOVED IN LIFE.

A GALLERY OF FAMOUS GHOSTS

There are many world-famous ghosts, which as a ghost hunter, you should to be familiar with. Here is just a short list to start you off.

ANNE BOLEYN (HAUNTER)

Second of the eight ill-fated wives of King Henry VIII, she was beheaded when she failed to produce a male heir. Her ghost is believed to pace the corridors of the Tower of London, where a few people claim to have seen her carrying her head under her arm!

THE GHOSTS OF CHRISTMAS PAST, PRESENT, AND FUTURE (MESSAGE-BRINGERS)

In *A Christmas Carol*, these three spirits visit Mr. Scrooge on Christmas Eve to convince him to take a long, hard look at his life and change for the better. You might be motivated too if a creepy hooded ghost showed you your own tombstone!

GHOST OF THE POLISH AIRMAN (MESSAGE-BRINGER)

During World War II, a bomber plane crashed into a bog near a British airbase in Lincolnshire, England, killing the five Polish crewmembers aboard. For 40 years afterward, people walking near the bog often me a man dressed in a WWII flier's uniform who spoke to them in a foreign language. On those days, the distinctive tail of a bomber was often seen disappearing into the bog. In the 1980s, workers in the bog found the wreckage of the plane, and buried the remains of the crew. No ghostly planes or pilots were seen there again.

GHOST OF GEORGE WASHINGTON (AVENGER)

During the United States Civil War, Union soldiers were battling Confederate troops at Gettysburg, Pennsylvania, when a figure appeared before them. It was an officer on a white stallion with a flaming sword, dressed in the uniform of the American Revolution. It was the ghost of George Washington, who then called out the command, "Fix bayonets! Charge!" The Union soldiers charged down the hill and forced the Confederates into a full retreat. Current Gettysburg residents say that sometimes on hot summer nights they still see a ghostly rider on a beautiful white horse galloping across the battlefield.

ALWAYS MAKE SURE TO WASH YOUR HANDS BEFORE ATTENDING A SEANCE.

CHAPTER THREE

GHOST DETECTION

Since ghosts are no longer really part of the material world and are often invisible as well, it can be difficult to detect them. Ghost hunters have developed special techniques for sensing the presence of a ghost and observing its actions. Without these, a person could be surrounded by ghosts and never know it!

Ghosts do not always want to be noticed; some ghosts are not interested in having anything to do with living people at all. But just because a ghost doesn't want to be noticed doesn't mean that people near it won't catch on to the fact that something weird is going on. In fact, the living often sense the presence of ghosts but don't know quite what they are experiencing—and that's where ghost hunters really come in handy.

So how does a ghost hunter decide whether a ghost may be present? By assembling a ghost-hunter's field kit and using the ghost detection methods described in this chapter.

THE GHOST HUNTER'S FIELD KIT

Like any professional, a ghost hunter needs to keep certain pieces of equipment handy to get the job done right.

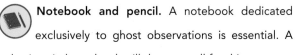 **Notebook and pencil.** A notebook dedicated exclusively to ghost observations is essential. A basic spiral notebook will do very well for this purpose.

For each possible encounter, note the date, time, location, and any special circumstances. Write down everything you see, hear, and feel. Don't wait—record your observations as soon as you have them. It's surprisingly easy to forget exactly what happened, particularly when your adrenaline is flowing. Write down where you are, who is with you, and exactly what you're experiencing.

A thermometer. A thermometer is always part of a well-equipped ghost hunter's kit. Use it to take the temperature in various spots around any possibly haunted locations. Be sure to get the kind that's used to measure air temperature—the ones used to take body temperature aren't sensitive enough.

A camera. Another must-have. Any kind of camera will do, but many ghost hunters prefer to use

instant cameras so the pictures can be examined without waiting for the film to be developed.

A tape recorder. Necessary for capturing ghostly
noises. A handheld tape recorder with a "voice-
activation" feature is best. This type of tape recorder
will start recording only when there is noise, saving the
ghost hunter from listening to hours and hours of blank
tape before hearing any sounds.

A compass. Useful for detecting ghost "hot spots"
in a haunted place. Make sure to record any locations where the compass needle starts spinning or
twitching. Strange behavior from a compass means the
magnetic field is being affected unusually, which is often
a sign that a ghost is present.

Colleagues. It's almost impossible to accomplish
ghost detection all alone; bring along at least one

other person, and preferably more, to help. Even if your companions aren't experienced ghost hunters themselves, they can back up your observations, and keep you from getting lonely or bored—or frightened! Remember to have someone present who doesn't know the history of the hauntings, for independent verification.

GHOST DETECTION METHODS

There are four basic tools in the ghost hunter's bag of tricks: observation, measurement, recording, and verification. First, it is necessary to learn as much as possible about the nature of the ghost under investigation; second, it is important to try to detect the ghost scientifically; third, it is extremely important to obtain concrete, physical evidence of the ghost's existence; and fourth, it is crucial to have independent accounts of the detection.

OBSERVATION

Observation is, quite simply, watching and listening. The hard part of good observation is to start without any preconceived notions—that is, already existing ideas—about what you might see. If you start your investigation thinking you're going to see a floating clown head, the odds are good you'll see a floating clown head. Have you heard of the power of suggestion? (see p. 56) Even seasoned ghost

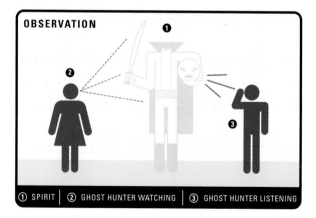

OBSERVATION

① SPIRIT | ② GHOST HUNTER WATCHING | ③ GHOST HUNTER LISTENING hunters are not immune. So try to be objective and open to whatever you see, hear, or feel.

A good ghost hunter never works alone but always has witnesses to back up the report. It's also a good idea to bring along a witness who is clueless about details of the haunting. A person who has no ideas about the strange phenomena to be investigated will be objective, which means they can report exactly what they see instead of what they thought they were going to see. That's important for getting independent verification. That's just one reason to work in a group. It's also helpful to have other people to carry some equipment. Then you'll also have someone to talk to. Sitting around waiting for ghosts can get boring! (Also, hanging around creepy, possibly haunted houses by yourself probably isn't going to be such a good idea.)

MEASUREMENT

Taking scientific measurements to detect a ghost's presence is a common procedure for professional ghost hunters. Ghosts often leave physical evidence of their presence. Some of the measurable phenomena include:

① **Temperature changes.** The presence of a ghost is often accompanied by a temperature change—usually a dramatic drop. If this can be measured—either by monitoring the room and recording the temperatures as they change, or by recording different temperatures in the same area—it will provide some evidence of a ghost's presence, even if no one sees or hears anything unusual.

② **Magnetic field changes.** As you may have learned in science class, the earth has magnetic poles—the North and South Poles—and a compass needle will point to

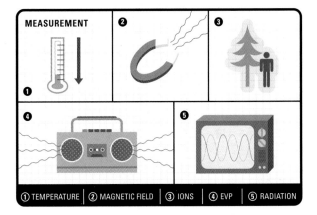

one and away from the other. Ghosts can cause fluctuation in the magnetic field around them—so the best way to detect such an event is with a compass. A fluctuation will cause a compass needle to spin or wobble wildly.

③ **Fluctuations in the ion field.** Ions are charged particles in the air that occur naturally everywhere, forming an ion field that surrounds everything. It is thought that the presence of ghosts reverses the ions' charges, disturbing the ion field. Such disturbances have been known to make ghost hunters break out in goose-bumps—but a more scientific way to measure is with an ion field counter.

④ **Electronic Voice Phenomena (EVP).** Some ghost phe-nomena can be heard only on recorded tape. Ghost hunters have sat taping for hours in rooms where not a sound was heard—but when the tape was played back, ghostly sounds had been recorded!

⑤ **Radiation.** Electro-magnetic radiation comes in many forms, including light, microwaves, radio waves, X-rays, and television signal waves. There is so much of this around us all the time that it blends together into a sort of background noise of electromagnetic radiation, which the presence of a ghost may disturb. A Gauss meter is a kind of instrument used only by professional ghost hunters that measures changes in this background radiation.

There are other kinds of measurements that can be taken, but these are the basics. If you can detect a measurable change in the surroundings, a change that has no visible or logical cause, then a ghost may be present, even if you can't see or hear it.

RECORDING

The ultimate goal of every ghost hunter is to obtain solid physical evidence of a ghost. This isn't as easy as it sounds. Many totally ordinary things can be mistaken for ghostly phenomena. A white streak resembling a ghostly energy trail could just be light bouncing off a camera strap that fell in front of the lens. On videotape, sunlight glinting off a passing bug can turn an ordinary housefly into "evidence"

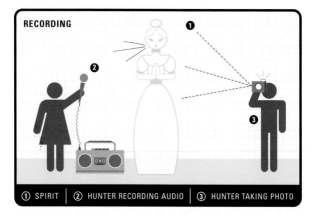

RECORDING

① SPIRIT | ② HUNTER RECORDING AUDIO | ③ HUNTER TAKING PHOTO

of a spectral presence! There have been cases of dishonest people faking ghost photographs, so the conscientious ghost hunter has to be especially careful.

Always take a photograph whenever there is suspicion that a ghost may be present, even if there seems to be nothing there! Similarly, if a room shows signs of being haunted, set up a tape recorder to see if it can pick up any EVP.

If something shows up on film or tape in the same place where you measured a temperature change or in the same room where the family always sees a ghost, that's good evidence.

Keep in mind that the existence of ghosts probably can't be proven beyond a doubt—but it is still possible to gather some good evidence that supports their existence.

VERIFICATION

Verification, or evidence that the weird incidents are truly caused by a ghost and not something much more commonplace—like a mischievous puppy or a prank-playing little brother—is an important concept for every ghost hunter. Not all ghost sightings are real, and many seemingly supernatural occurrences can be explained logically. A tree branch rubbing against a window can make an eerie scratching noise. A freezing water pipe can make a moaning noise. Someone just waking up from a dream can see things that aren't really there, but not because they're seeing a ghost. Ghost hunters need to be able to rule out all rational explanations for strange phenomena before concluding that a ghost is at the root of it all!

One thing to watch out for is the "power of suggestion." Let's say that Jenny and Jules both live in a house that may be haunted. Jules has seen a semitranslucent, grayish-colored lady walking down the hallway, and he's told Jenny all about it. If Jenny sees the gray lady too, that might be because she expects to see it after hearing Jules's story. If Jenny had seen the gray lady without knowing what Jules saw, that would make for much stronger evidence in favor of the ghost's existence. When a ghost hunter records the same story from several different people—without any of them having previously heard about it or talked to anyone else who saw it—that is called "independent verification," and it's something a serious ghost hunter needs to have. Independent verification often comes from guests who stay in a haunted house and see something that the family members have all seen—except that the guests didn't know the story before their visit.

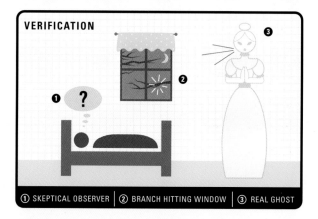

VERIFICATION

① SKEPTICAL OBSERVER | ② BRANCH HITTING WINDOW | ③ REAL GHOST

ALWAYS REMAIN CALM WHEN ENCOUNTERING A GHOST. EVEN FAMOUS GHOSTS

CHAPTER FOUR

WHAT TO DO IF YOU ENCOUNTER A GHOST

Finding and identifying a ghost are essential aspects of a ghost hunter's task, but what is the right thing to do upon actually encountering one? The following pages explain the ghost hunter's main responsibilities when meeting a ghost.

SECURING THE AREA

First, ask everyone to leave. You and your team should be alone in the location when you're investigating. Be sure not to forget pets—a frightened dog or cat could complicate things considerably.

Second, make a detailed search. Move quietly and slowly. Look for cold spots and areas where the compass needle goes crazy. Concentrate on locations where the ghosts have been seen or heard. If you detect any fluctuations, write them down at once and take some pictures. It is also a good idea to record the entire search on audiotape. A lot of ghost hunters like to draw a map of the house, and mark on the map the location of any unusual observations.

Third, once the sweep is finished, set up camp in an area where paranormal occurrences have happened. With notebook and recording tools handy, get comfortable, and then wait. Remember to begin the investigation at the time of day when most of the previous sightings occurred.

KEEPING RECORDS

Write down everything! Anything that seems unusual—anything you see, hear, or feel—could prove to be important later when it is time to analyze the data. Stay alert and try not to get distracted. This isn't the time for an intense game of Monopoly or writing in your diary! Remember, this is a scientific investigation and it needs your full attention.

COMMUNICATING WITH GHOSTS

A cold, damp wind blows through your observation post (even though you're indoors), the compass needle whirls wildly, and a misty vapor hovers in the air in front of you. Congratulations, you've found a ghost! Now what?

Should you try to communicate with it? This is not always possible, nor might you even want to. If a renegade poltergeist is hurling things at you, there is only one thing to do: run! You can always come back later when things have calmed down.

Most ghost encounters will not be nearly so clear, however; many times it may not be certain that a ghost is present at all. If you suspect that a spectral being is in the vicinity, do not attempt to communicate with it immediately. The first steps should be to observe, record, and measure. If the ghostly presence remains or recurs and you've gathered as much information as you can about it, that's the right time to try communicating.

Not all ghosts are capable of communication. Many ghost hunters have observed that a majority of ghosts seem to be rather single-minded, locked into one particular task or activity. This might not include speaking or writing. Ghosts often ignore people who approach them or try to speak to them, as if they don't even see them there. Even message-bringer ghosts often only communicate one-way. They can speak to you, but they don't hear you or respond if you speak to them. They're not being rude; two-way communication just isn't in their nature. You might not feel like talking either if you were stuck between worlds and could only lurk around someone else's basement or spare bedroom night after night.

However, it may be worth trying to get a ghost talking. Some ghosts, even poltergeists (typically the least chatty type of ghost), will communicate with people. Here are some approaches to try:

① **Look directly at the ghost.** Don't stare at the floor or the ceiling. Ghosts are used to people running away from them or covering their eyes in fright. Be different; you may arouse the ghost's curiosity.

② **Try not to show fear.** You might be feeling a little uneasy (you're only human, after all), but ghosts are often very sensitive to fear in others. Some enjoy inspiring fear, others feel bad that people are afraid of them. The safest way for you to behave is as if the ghost is just another person you're meeting for the first time. So try to look calm, relaxed, and ready for a heart-to-heart chat.

③ **Speak directly to the ghost.** Address it politely and state your purpose. It may be able to respond; if not, it may show some signs that it can hear and understand you, which is something.

④ **Write to the ghost.** People have sometimes communicated with ghosts by writing messages on paper or even on the walls, and leaving them for the ghost to see. Ideally, the ghost will write a reply. This has, on occasion, worked to establish some level of communication. There can be problems, however. If the ghost doesn't speak the same language as the person leaving messages, or if the ghost is unable to read or write (often a problem with the ghosts of long-dead people), this technique is doomed to failure. A real catastrophe is when the ghost's handwriting is too messy to read!

⑤ **Try using code.** This often works with poltergeists. If a ghost cannot speak, it may be able to communicate some other way. If the ghost often raps on the walls, try asking it questions and telling it to rap once for yes, twice for no. In this way a whole system of code can be worked out. Try to imagine other ways to set up communication codes that don't depend on speaking or writing.

⑥ **Last resort: use a toy.** This might not seem the most scientific method, but sometimes if all else fails, some of the more traditional ghost-communication toys, such as Ouija boards or Magic 8 Balls, will elicit a response. Keep in mind that a message you get from a ghost this way might not be very reliable—or even from the ghost. These toys usually respond more to the person using them than to any ghost who might be hanging around.

COMMUNICATING WITH GHOSTS

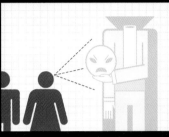

① LOOK DIRECTLY AT THE GHOST

② TRY NOT TO SHOW FEAR

③ SPEAK DIRECTLY TO THE GHOST

④ WRITE TO THE GHOST

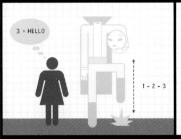

⑤ TRY USING CODE

⑥ USE A TOY (MAGIC 8 BALL, OUIJA, ETC.)

HOW NOT TO BE SCARED: It's human nature to be afraid of ghosts, and you're probably no different. Not to worry. It's okay to be a little scared, but as a ghost hunter you don't want to be seen running from the haunted location screaming. Here are some tips to keep the willies away:

Keep your friends close by • Keep a flashlight handy • Whistle or hum a favorite tune • Stay focused on what you're doing • Think of it as a scientific experiment • Smile if you see a ghost

CONVERSING WITH GHOSTS

Everyone has experienced the feeling of being tongue-tied or unsure of what to say in an unusual situation. What is the right thing to say to a ghost? Well, that's a tricky question. Generally, it's a good idea to start with some sort of friendly greeting, to let the ghost know you have good intentions. Next, try to find out who the ghost was in life. Once that has been established, ask why the ghost is still around, and what, if anything, it wants.

Be prepared for confusing answers. The ghost may not fully realize what it has become and what it is doing there. It may still think it's alive, or that it's still the year it died, and it may not even know exactly why it's still around. There are instances of investigators establishing long dialogues with ghosts in which they learned a great deal, but there are just as many instances of investigators who managed to talk to a ghost but ended up even more confused. It will all depend on the ghost you're speaking to.

A mischief-maker ghost will probably not have anything useful to say. A ghost like this is mostly interested in causing trouble and scaring people—in fact, it might even be annoyed that you're not shrieking and running away!

A message-bringer may stick strictly to the message it is supposed to bring and say nothing else. While this is frustrating, and you may have to listen to its message a number of times (getting pretty sick of it in the process), once it understands that you've received the message, you might be able to get some other information out of it.

The best chance for interesting conversation is probably with an avenger ghost. It may just be dying to tell you the story of its wrongful death and what it wants!

WHAT IF THE GHOST IS UNFRIENDLY?

Despite what scary books and horror movies portray, the truth is that ghosts are rarely mean or hostile. People get scared upon seeing a ghost, but it's usually only because they are startled. Remember that ghosts have no real substance, and they can't hurt you.

Watch out for poltergeists, however. They can throw things around—and there are even cases of people being scratched or slapped! If a poltergeist throws a vase across the room and it hits you, it'll hurt. The best advice is to stay well out of the way until the disturbance stops. If you can communicate with a poltergeist, politely ask it to stop. It may not realize it's causing such trouble.

POLTERGEISTS CAN BE MOODY. WATCH OUT!

TIPS FOR THE TONGUE-TIED HUNTER

Stumped about what to say to a ghost? It's easy to feel uncomfortable. What do you say to someone who might have been dead for decades? Here are a few ideas to get you started on the road to meaningful communication with a ghost.

"How long have you lived here?"

"Where are you from?"

"Do you know what year it is?"

"Do you live here, or are you just visiting?"

"Why are you here?"

"Do you have a message for us?"

GHOST ERADICATION

Although this isn't really your job, you may be asked to help get rid of the pesky ghosts. Some ghosts are friendly and people don't mind having them around, but a resident ghost isn't always part of the average family's dream home.

In this situation, the best you can do is to try to find out what the ghost wants or needs, and help it if you can. This works especially well with an avenger ghost. Even if the person who wronged the spook was never punished, just telling the ghost that its story will be heard might help. Reassure it that you'll try to get the word out about the injustice that's been done.

A message-bringer may need reassurance that its message has been received. Once convinced, it may go away by itself. Especially if it has been around for a long time, repeating the same message over and over again, it might be ecstatic at finally being heard!

A mischief-making specter may not realize the harm it is doing; it may simply be having fun. Ask it to stop, or suggest an alternative location, and the disturbances may stop.

Even if there is no way to help the ghost or answer its questions, remember that it's still a ghost-hunter's primary responsibility to prove the existence of ghosts, not chase

SOME GHOSTS CAN BE VERY SHY.

them away or destroy them. After all, a ghost has a right to exist, too. And it was probably there first!

CREATING A CASE HISTORY

Finally, after every ghost encounter it is essential to create a case history. This will require a ghost hunter to compile many different kinds of evidence, including eyewitness accounts from people who have seen the ghost or interacted with it, scientific measurements, and, if possible, audio or video recordings of the ghost.

The first step is to build up a good history of the house or building, the land, and the people who've lived there. Here are some important elements in a useful case history:

• **Witness statements.** Gather as many witness statements as possible. Try to talk to anyone who's experienced the haunting. This includes the people who live in the house, former residents who've moved away, friends and guests who stayed in the house, workers who've done work inside, and any other ghost hunters who have already investigated the house.

• **History of the building.** Find out when the house was built, if it's been changed or altered significantly, and its history. Was it always a house? Was it once a nursing home, or a bed-and-breakfast? More importantly, has anyone died in the house? Has anyone who lived in the house died a particularly traumatic or violent death, even if that death didn't occur inside the house?

• **History of the land.** Find out, if you can, about the land where the house was built. Was it once used for another purpose? Was the land used as a graveyard or execution site? Was it a campground, playground, or hiking area?

- **Alternative explanations.** This will require some detective work. Any good ghost hunter will look for an ordinary explanation for the occurrences before moving on to supernatural possibilities. If people hear scratching at the window, is there a tree outside with branches that might be scraping? If there are spooky footsteps heard in an apartment, is there a staircase outside or heavy-footed people who live above? Remember, a good ghost hunter is a good detective!

THERE GOES THE NEIGHBORHOOD!

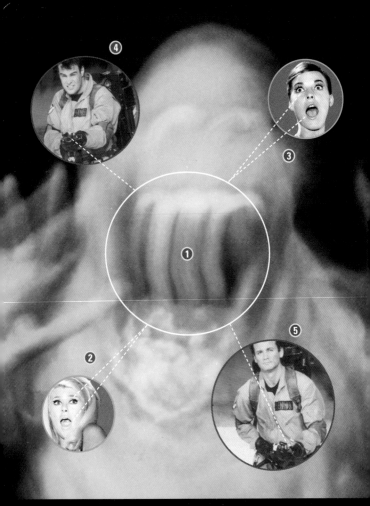

① GHOST   ② ③ GHOST OBSERVERS

④ ⑤ GHOST HUNTERS

CHAPTER FIVE

CONCLUSION

There's no magical secret code for ghost hunters, no ancient mantra that will let you conjure up spirits at will and see them whenever you like. A ghost hunter is primarily a scientific investigator, and that's how you should think of yourself: as a scientist. A good scientist is objective and thorough.

Now that you've read this handbook, are you ready to be a ghost hunter? Can you wait patiently in a possibly haunted place, knowing that a ghost might be lurking around a corner? Can you look a ghost in the face and listen to what it has to say? If so, then you are ready to be a ghost hunter!

APPENDIX: FURTHER READING AND VIEWING

BOOKS

NONFICTION:

Coast to Coast Ghosts, by Leslie Rule

The Encyclopedia of Ghosts and Spirits, by Rosemary Ellen Guiley

The Everything Ghost Book, by Jason Rich

Ghost Sightings, by Brian Innes

Ghosts: True Encounters with the World Beyond, by Hans Holzer

Haunted America, by Michael Norman and Beth Scott

Here There Be Ghosts, by Jane Yolen

Mind Over Matter, by Loyd Auerbach

The Paranormal Sourcebook, by Charles Sellier

Relax, It's Only a Ghost, by Echo Bodine

Weird Science, by Michael White

FICTION:

The Canterville Ghost, by Oscar Wilde

A Christmas Carol, by Charles Dickens

Ghost Camp, by R. L. Stine

Ghost Soldier, by Elaine Marie Alphin

Ghost Story, by Peter Straub

The Ghost Chronicles, Volume I: User Friendly,
   by Lawrence Gordon

The Ghost Chronicles, Volume II: Haunted High,
   by Lawrence Gordon

The Ghost Followed Us Home, by Peg Kehret

Hamlet, by William Shakespeare

The Haunting of Hill House, by Shirley Jackson

The Hound of the Baskervilles, by Arthur Conan Doyle

The House with a Clock in Its Walls, by John Bellairs

The Legend of Sleepy Hollow, by Washington Irving

Rebecca, by Daphne Du Maurier

The Turn of the Screw, by Henry James

MOVIES

Beetlejuice, directed by Tim Burton (1988)

Blackbeard's Ghost, directed by Robert Stevenson (1968)

Blithe Spirit, directed by David Lean (1945)

The Canterville Ghost, directed by Jules Dassin (1944)

Casper, directed by Brad Silberling (1995)

Creeps, directed by Jules White (1956)

Curtain Call, directed by Peter Yates (1999)

Dead Men Tell, directed by Harry Lachman (1941)

Ghost, directed by Jerry Zucker (1990)

The Ghost and Mr. Chicken, directed by Alan Rafkin (1965)

The Ghost and Mrs. Muir, directed by Joseph L. Mankiewicz (1947)

The Ghost in the Invisible Bikini, directed by Don Weis (1966)

The Ghost of Greville Lodge, directed by Niall Johnson (2000)

Ghostbusters, directed by Ivan Reitman (1984)

Ghostbusters II, directed by Ivan Reitman (1989)

Ghost Wanted, directed by Chuck Jones (1940)

Gildersleeve's Ghost, directed by Gordon Douglas (1944)

Haunted Honeymoon, directed by Gene Wilder (1986)

The Haunting, directed by Robert Wise (1963)

The Others, directed by Alejandro Amenábar (2001)

Poltergeist, directed by Tobe Hooper (1982)

The Sixth Sense, directed by M. Night Shyamalan (1999)

Topper, directed by Norman Z. Macleod (1937)

Truly Madly Deeply, directed by Anthony Minghella (1991)

Windrunner, directed by William Clark and William Tannen
(1995)

GHOST HUNTER'S NOTEBOOK

❶

SIGHTING DATE:

SIGHTING TIME:

LOCATION:

TEMPERATURE:

STRANGE PHENOMENA OBSERVED, HEARD, FELT:

GHOST APPEARANCE:

GHOSTLY COMMUNICATION (IF ANY):

❷

SIGHTING DATE:

SIGHTING TIME:

LOCATION:

TEMPERATURE:

STRANGE PHENOMENA OBSERVED, HEARD, FELT:

GHOST APPEARANCE:

GHOSTLY COMMUNICATION (IF ANY):

❸

SIGHTING DATE:

SIGHTING TIME:

LOCATION:

TEMPERATURE:

STRANGE PHENOMENA OBSERVED, HEARD, FELT:

GHOST APPEARANCE:

GHOSTLY COMMUNICATION (IF ANY):

GHOST HUNTER IDENTIFICATION

IN SEARCH OF SPIRITS

The bearer of this ID has read and understood *The Ghost Hunter's Handbook*, and is thereby deemed fully competent to investigate and gather evidence regarding strange phenomena of the ghostly sort. Bearer should be granted unrestricted access to all sites of potential hauntings, including creepy old houses, misty graveyards, ancient battlegrounds, dusty attics, and places where things go bump in the night.

WARNING TO GHOSTS: Bearer is not easily frightened, so don't try any silly tricks.